Published by Hachette Partworks Ltd.
ISBN: 978-1-908648-55-6
Date of Printing: November 2012
Printed in Malaysia by Tien Wah Press

THE HUNCHBACK OF NOTRE DAME

Quasimodo To The Rescue

hachette

Long ago, in the city of
Paris, a bell ringer lived in
the tower of Notre Dame
cathedral. His name was
Quasimodo. He lived there
for many years with only
stone gargoyles for friends.
Their names were Victor,
Laverne and Hugo. And they
could only come to life for
Quasimodo.

Eventually, Quasimodo
made new friends in the
streets of Paris. But he still
lived in the bell tower, and
the gargoyles remained his
closest friends. Quasimodo
was always happy to greet
them each morning, when he
went to ring the bells to wake
the people of Paris.

BONG! BONG! BONG!
rang the bells.

When the bells stopped ringing, the
gargoyles complained to their friend.

"What a racket!" complained Hugo, the
plumpest gargoyle. "Why can't people
just get a rooster?"

"Yes," agreed Victor, the tallest
gargoyle. "That noise gives me a
headache."

Suddenly, Quasimodo heard the voice of another friend. It was Esmeralda. She was waving from the street below.

"I have a surprise for you, Quasimodo!" she called. "Lower your bucket!"

Quasimodo
lowered his bucket.
Esmeralda sent it
back up with a big,
juicy watermelon
inside!

"Esmeralda is so kind," said Quasimodo. He bit into a huge slice of watermelon.

But the gargoyles were still feeling grumpy.

"At least *she* thinks about her friends," said Laverne as she shooed away some pigeons. "Can't you do anything about these birds, Quasi?"

That night, as Quasimodo slept, a storm gathered. The dark sky lit up with lightning.

Victor, Laverne and Hugo began to shiver.

"It looks like rain," said Victor.

"Oh, I *hate* getting my wings wet," grumbled Hugo.

Suddenly, a bolt of lightning hit the bell tower.
Part of the railing fell away and the gargoyles
plunged down into the darkness below.

By morning, the storm had passed. The sun came out again, and the people of Paris awoke to find their city rinsed clean by the rain.

A farmer had left his horse and cart outside the cathedral. Now that the storm was over, he started off for home.

"Hmm, the wagon feels heavy," he said to his horse. "If I didn't know better, I'd say we had a load of watermelons in the back."

The farmer hadn't noticed that the gargoyles had fallen off the cathedral and landed in his cart!

Meanwhile, Quasimodo was getting ready to ring the bells. "Some storm last night!" he called to the gargoyles. There was no answer.

"Oh no!" cried Quasimodo. "My friends are gone!"

Quasimodo quickly guessed what had happened.
He ran down the tower steps as fast as he could.
"What's your hurry?" asked Esmeralda as
Quasimodo rushed past.

Quasimodo pointed to the bell tower. He told
Esmeralda about the three missing statues.

Esmeralda looked at Djali, her goat, who was nibbling some straw in the street. It gave her an idea.

"There was a cart right at this spot yesterday," she said. "Perhaps the statues fell into it! If we follow the trail of straw, I think we'll find them."

By then, the farmer had arrived home. He was just starting to load his cart with fresh watermelons when he saw the gargoyles.

"Monsters!" he cried, dropping
a melon on his foot.
"Don't panic," said his wife. "Look,
they're made of stone!"

Later that day, Quasimodo reached the end of the trail of straw.

"Hello," he called to the farmer. "Have you seen three statues?"

"I sold one of them to the blacksmith next door..." the farmer began.

Before the farmer could finish, Quasimodo rushed off to the blacksmith's forge.

The blacksmith was just about to pound a horseshoe on Victor's head when Quasimodo burst in.

"STOP!" he roared. But it was too late. Down came the hammer!

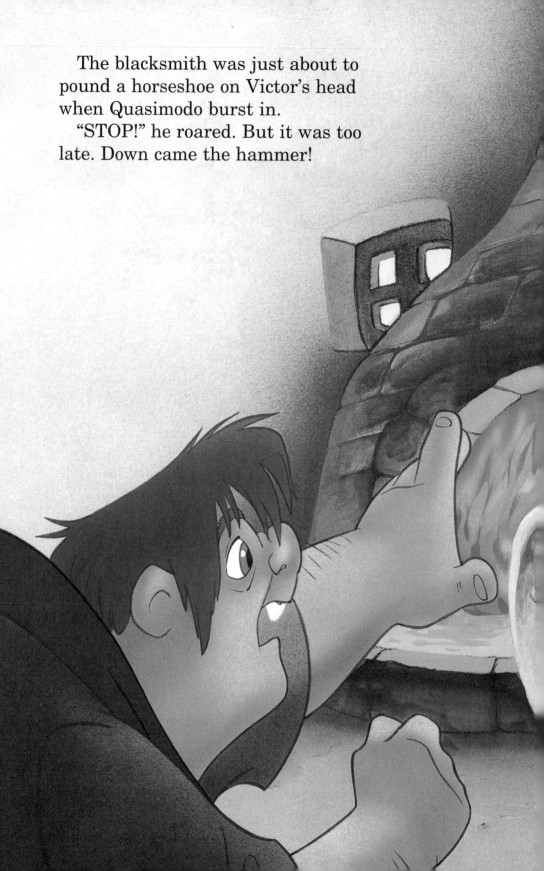

Quasimodo quickly paid the blacksmith for Victor and carried him back to the farmer's field.

"Now I've *really* got a headache," moaned Victor as he rubbed his head. "I'll never complain about the bells again!"

Quasimodo was glad to have Victor back. But where were the other two? He asked the farmer.

"A ship's captain wanted one of them," said the farmer. "His boat is on the river."

Quasimodo raced off to the river.

He arrived at the river bank just in time to see
Hugo about to be tossed overboard.
"STOP!" yelled Quasimodo.

But it was too late.
SPLASH! Hugo was hurled into the water.

Without thinking, Quasimodo
dived into the river to save his
friend. He knew how much Hugo
hated water!

Quasimodo dived down to the river bed.
Poor Hugo was stuck in the mud, next to
an old ship's anchor. Quasimodo tugged
and pulled until he finally
freed Hugo.

"How dare you steal my anchor!" the captain
shouted at Quasimodo.

"It's not an anchor, it's my statue," explained
Quasimodo. "But don't worry, I'll get you a better
anchor for your ship."

Quasimodo placed Hugo carefully on the deck, and dived back into the water.

He dragged the old anchor out of the mud.

"That ugly old statue wasn't much good as an anchor, anyway," grunted the ship's captain.

"Who's he calling ugly?" spluttered Hugo as
Quasimodo carried him back to the farm.

Quasimodo put Hugo down beside Victor, then asked the farmer about the third statue. The farmer pointed to his watermelon patch.

"See for yourself," said the farmer. "I thought that ugly statue would make a good scarecrow, but I was wrong – those pesky birds seem to like it! Take it back if you want to."

It was true. All the crows were indeed
flocking round Laverne.

"Looks like you've made some new friends," Quasimodo said to Laverne. He chuckled at the flock of crows flying round her head.

"Just get me out of here!" hissed Laverne. "Now, please!"

The kind farmer let Quasimodo use his cart
to take the statues back to the cathedral. Victor,
Laverne and Hugo sat in the back, as still as
statues should be.

The sun was setting by the time Quasimodo and his friends arrived back in Paris. Esmeralda watched as Quasimodo carefully hoisted the gargoyles back up to their places on the bell tower.

"Thank you for rescuing us, Quasi," said Victor.

"Yes, but I do think we should get out to the countryside more often," said Hugo.

"You've got rocks in your head," Laverne scolded Hugo. "At least the city birds have some manners. Their country cousins have no respect for age or beauty! Not like our friend, Quasimodo."

Quasimodo laughed. He was so happy to have his friends back home, even if they were as grumpy as ever!